SCANDINAVIA

RUSSIA

AND

UTAIN

EUROPE

MIDDLE EAST

CHINA

ARABIA

INDIA

AFRICA

AUSTRALIA

NEW ZEALAND

ANTARCTICA

For my niece Pamela and her family: It was when we
visited you in Uganda that I fell in love with giraffes, and
the idea for this story was born.

—A.M.

For my growing family, and with thanks to my dear
friend Ainslie, whose warm encouragement inspired me
to illustrate *A Giraffe Called Geranium*.

—M.B.

Published in 2014 by Red Diamond Books | www.reddiamondbooks.ca
Text © 2014 Ainslie Manson
Illustrations © 2014 Mary Baker

Library and Archives Canada Cataloguing in Publication

Manson, Ainslie, author
A giraffe called Geranium / written by Ainslie Manson ; illustrated
by Mary Baker.
ISBN 978-0-9937341-0-6 (bound), ISBN 978-0-9937341-1-3 (pbk.)
1. Giraffe--Juvenile fiction. I. Baker, Mary, 1950-, illustrator
II. Title.
PS8576.A567G57 2014   jC813'.54   C2014-902811-3

A "tree–free book"
Printed and bound in Manitoba, Canada, by Friesens

Edited by Tiffany Stone
Book design by Heather Lohnes and Amy Williams

10 9 8 7 6 5 4 3 2 1

A Giraffe Called GERANIUM

Written by
AINSLIE MANSON

Illustrated by
MARY BAKER

RD RED DIAMOND BOOKS

One warm summer day, on the west coast of Canada, a young giraffe stepped gracefully over Susanna's gate and into her garden. Susanna could hardly believe her eyes. Giraffes were her favourite animal! She didn't even mind when it began eating her prized geraniums.

"Welcome," she said softly, removing a frayed rope from around the giraffe's neck. "Have you come all the way from Africa?"

The giraffe munched happily on another flower.

Susanna smiled. "I think I'll call you Geranium."

Before long, the last flower in Susanna's garden was hanging from Geranium's mouth.

"Let's find you something better to eat," said Susanna.

At the bottom of the garden, Geranium reached high into the branches of a pear tree. Within minutes, there were no pears left. No leaves either. Neighbours stared over the fence in disbelief.

"Perhaps it's time to take you inside," said Susanna.

It took a great deal of pushing and pulling to get Geranium through the front door. And when she was finally inside, she was unable to stand up straight.

So Susanna cut a hole in the ceiling. "Now you can stretch out your long neck," she said, "and when you do, your head will be in my bedroom."

Geranium had an enormous appetite, and over the weeks that followed, Susanna had to order truckloads of vegetables. She fed Geranium in the bedroom, so the giraffe wouldn't have to bend over. It was hard work hauling all the vegetables upstairs.

Onions turned out to be Geranium's favourite. She often had onion breath, which didn't seem fitting for a giraffe called Geranium.

Geranium spent most of her days eating and most of her nights chewing her cud beside Susanna's bed. It was wonderful when she put her head down on Susanna's pillow and actually slept.

Everything that went into Geranium soon came out. Each morning, with a clothes-peg on her nose, Susanna had to scrub the front hall.

"Maybe if I walked you three times a day," she said, "you could learn to go outside?"

However, Geranium caused nothing but trouble on her walks.

On her first walk, she spied a neighbour's apple tree.

"Hey!" the neighbour called out. "Get away from there! Those are my apples!"

"Come, Geranium," said Susanna.

But Geranium reached for another apple instead.

The next day was worse.

"That giraffe tried to eat my bag!" said the mailman. "It belongs in a zoo!"

"I agree," said an angry woman. "All my lovely roses have gone down its gullet!"

Susanna pretended she hadn't heard.

At the end of each giraffe-filled day, Susanna was exhausted. Often she could only curl up in a chair and watch TV. Geranium watched too. She seemed to like nature programs the best, especially if they were about her homeland, Africa. But after watching them, she always looked sad.

Autumn came, then winter. Geranium's head drooped,
and she shivered from the cold. Even hugs didn't help.
Nothing seemed to cheer her up. Not even onions.

When a snowstorm howled around the house one night, Susanna was woken up by an unusual sound.

"Baaaaa!" cried Geranium. This was her first word! But it was a heartbreaking cry, like a lost lamb would make.

"Oh, Geranium, please don't be sad," said Susanna, stroking the giraffe tenderly. "I think I know a way to get you home."

A familiar sailboat was moored in the cove. Susanna had known the captain all her life. She had heard he was about to set sail and was looking for crew.

"My friend Geranium and I would be happy to be your crew if we could take her home to Africa," she said.

The captain agreed.

But he almost changed his mind when he met Geranium. "Accommodation will be tight," he said.

It took some coaxing to get Geranium aboard.

"Don't worry," said Susanna. "I'm coming too."

"Batten down the hatches," said the captain. "Winds willing, we'll be there in no time."

The winds were willing, but they were wild.

"Shiver me timbers!" said the captain when the mast blew down. "Now what will we do?"

"Look!" said Susanna. "Geranium has saved the day!"

"Thank you, Geranium," said the captain. "You will make a marvellous mast until we can find a suitable tree for a new one."

Geranium was an excellent lookout. When they needed to stretch, she found white sand beaches for them to run on. When they were hungry and thirsty, she found islands with fruit trees and fresh water.

Eventually, she even found Africa...and nearly capsized the boat in her excitement.

Geranium set off at a gallop, with Susanna racing after her. It was almost impossible to keep up.

Just when Susanna knew she couldn't run another step, they came upon a herd of giraffes.

She held her breath as one walked slowly toward Geranium. The two touched noses, then tenderly pressed their necks together. Geranium had found a friend.

By the time the captain caught up, the whole herd, including Geranium, had their long necks high in the acacia trees, feasting.

"It's like a welcoming party!" said Susanna.
     The captain nodded, and together they gazed in wonder
at the giraffes as the sky slowly turned orange.

When the sun began to set, Susanna knew it was time to go. Geranium left the herd and came to her. She nudged Susanna gently.

Susanna wrapped her arms around the giraffe's neck. "I'm so happy to see you running wild and free. It makes leaving you a little easier."

She felt giraffe breath on her cheek and received a farewell lick.

"Goodbye, Geranium," said Susanna. "Living with you was always an adventure! I'll smile whenever I think of you. And I'll think of you every day."

She watched Geranium gallop back through the golden grass to her new friends and knew that one day she would come back to visit her.

As she and the captain walked back to the boat,

Susanna began to plan...

Did you know?

When a giraffe calf is born, it is as tall and as heavy as a full-grown human.

An adult giraffe can grow to six metres (20 feet). That's taller than three men standing on each other's heads! But a full-grown giraffe can weigh as much as 1,361 kilograms (3,000 pounds), about five times more than three men would weigh!

Giraffes' leathery black tongues are as long as a human's arm. Giraffes can use their tongues like enormous cotton swabs to clean inside their own ears.

No two giraffes have the exact same pattern of spots. Their spots help to hide them from predators. When near shrubbery, they blend in with the shadows and sunlight.

Giraffes don't like to swim. Their long necks make them top-heavy. But giraffes have been found in places they could only have reached by swimming. So it is believed that they will swim when they have to.

Long ago, giraffes were frequently stolen from Africa and sold to zoos around the world. Nowadays, it would be extremely difficult to smuggle a giraffe out of the country. However, giraffes are still under threat in Africa. They are poached (illegally hunted) for food, for their beautiful skins, and for their long tail hairs.

CANADA

USA

ATLANTIC
OCEAN

PACIFIC
OCEAN

AMAZON
RIVER

SOUTH
AMERICA

Geranium's Voyage
Home